PAULA DANZIGER
Amber Brown
Treasury

illustrated by Tony Ross

Previously published as
It's a Fair Day, Amber Brown,
Get Ready for Second Grade, Amber Brown
and What a Trip Amber Brown.

Putnam
an imprint of Penguin Young Readers Group

G. P. PUTNAM'S SONS
A division of Penguin Young Readers Group
Published by The Penguin Group.
Penguin Young Readers Group, 345 Hudson Street, New York, New York 10014, U.S.A.
Penguin Group (Canada), 90 Eglinton Avenue East, Suite 700,
Toronto, Ontario, Canada M4P 2Y3 (a division of Pearson Penguin Canada Inc.).
Penguin Books Ltd, 80 Strand, London WC2R 0RL, England.
Penguin Ireland, 25 St Stephen's Green, Dublin 2, Ireland (a division of Penguin Books Ltd).
Penguin Group (Australia), 250 Camberwell Road, Camberwell, Victoria 3124,
Australia (a division of Pearson Australia Group Pty Ltd).
Penguin Books India Pvt Ltd, 11 Community Centre,
Panchsheel Park, New Delhi - 110 017, India.
Penguin Group (NZ), 67 Apollo Drive, Rosedale, North Shore 0632,
New Zealand (a division of Pearson New Zealand Ltd).
Penguin Books (South Africa) (Pty) Ltd, 24 Sturdee Avenue,
Rosebank, Johannesburg 2196, South Africa.
Registered Offices: Penguin Books Ltd, 80 Strand, London WC2R 0RL, England.

Originally published as
It's a Fair Day, Amber Brown,
978-0-399-23606-8
Get Ready for Second Grade, Amber Brown,
978-0-399-23607-5
What A Trip, Amber Brown,
978-0-399-23469-9

Text copyright © Paula Danziger, 2001, 2002
Illustrations copyright © Tony Ross, 2001, 2002

Special Markets ISBN 978-0-399-25552-6

1 3 5 7 9 10 8 6 4 2

It's a Fair Day,
Amber Brown

I, Amber Brown, wake up

and hope that today is going to be a perfect day.

Yesterday was not a perfect day.

My mom and dad were angry at each other.

I, Amber Brown, hate when that happens.

I get dressed.

I put on all my good-luck things

to start a perfect vacation day.

As I walk downstairs,

I make sure that the back of my right shoe

touches each step.

When it touches each step, I say,

"Perfect day, perfect day."

Everyone is already in the kitchen,

talking and laughing—

Mom, Dad, my best friend, Justin Daniels,

his parents and his little brother, Danny.

We are all staying together in the Poconos.

Justin and I call it the Poke-a-Nose.

It looks like the beginning of a perfect day.

I pick up the box of Crunchie Munchies,
my favorite cereal.

It feels empty. I shake it. No sound.

I look inside. It's empty. I look inside again.

"Someone's eaten all of my cereal."

"Goldilocks and the three bears," Danny yells.

Everyone laughs except me.

What if not having my favorite cereal

means that today is not going to be a perfect day?

I, Amber Brown, look at the table.

Justin's bowl is overflowing with Crunchie Munchies.

Justin burps.

"Justin," his mother says.

I cross my eyes at him and oink.

He makes a funny face.

I oink again.

He makes another funny face.

I bet that he thinks I am going to just forget

that he's eaten all of my cereal . . .

and maybe ruined a perfect day.

Well, he's not only a pig. He's a pig in trouble.

"I wanted to eat some and then make a necklace
out of some of them," I say.

"Girls." Justin puts a spoonful of
Crunchie Munchies in his mouth.

He reaches over and takes food off Danny's plate.

"Why don't you just make a necklace
out of toaster waffles?"

Sometimes he just drives me nuts.

At home in New Jersey,

Justin and I are best friends.

We live next door to each other.

I am an only child.

Here in the Poconos,

we are all in the same house

and I don't feel like an only child.

Justin slurps the milk in his bowl.

I make myself a peanut butter

and jelly sandwich . . .

and ignore Justin.

Danny twirls around the room,

pretending to be a top.

I ignore him too.

My dad stands up.

"I'll go to the store and pick up

more Crunchie Munchies for Amber."

"Philip. Sit down," my mother says.

"I know what you are up to.

You want to go to the grocery store

so that you can call work.

This is your vacation. Relax."

My dad sits down again and sighs.

I sit down and start eating my sandwich.

Justin looks at me and crosses his eyes.

I cross my eyes back at him.

Then I look at my parents.

My dad looks as if he is trying hard

to stay in his seat and not call the office.

My mom looks as if she's trying hard

not to be annoyed that my dad

wants to call the office on his vacation.

But I know she is.

I cross my fingers and make a wish

that my parents don't get into a fight.

Then I put my head down on the table.

I hear the sound of something

scraping across the table toward me.

I lift my head and look.

It is the rest of Justin's cereal.

"Let's share," he says.

"I'll eat a toaster waffle instead."

The bowl is filled with soggy cereal.

I, Amber Brown, like to put a little milk on top

and eat it fast while it is still crispy.

My mom passes the bowl back to Justin.

"That's very nice of you, Justin,

but it's not very healthy."

It's a good thing that my mom doesn't know

that sometimes at school,

Justin and I share a piece of bubble gum . . .

after it has already been in one of our mouths.

I smile at Justin slurping milk out of his bowl.

He smiles back.

Justin's dad says, "Let's hurry up.

We should leave soon for the fair."

The county fair . . . rides and games and lots of food.

I, Amber Brown, am so excited.

"Look, Danny," I say, "that sign says

'Welcome to the County Fair.'"

"I can count." Danny jumps up and down.

"One, two, seven, four, eleven."

"County." I try to explain. "Not counting."

"County! County!" Danny jumps up and down aga

"One-y, two-y, seven-y, four-y, eleven-y."

Justin looks at his little brother.

"Garbanzo-bean brain."

"Justin," Mr. Daniels says. "No name-calling."

We go into the fair.

"Cotton candy!" Danny runs over to the booth.

We all follow.

"I'll buy one for each of us," my dad says.

"That stuff is disgusting," my mom says.

My dad buys it anyway.

My mom throws hers in the garbage.

Suddenly, my cotton candy doesn't taste so good.

We go to the barns.

The animals are cute, but the barn stinks . . .

sort of like Danny when he needs

to have his diaper changed.

Like now.

"Look at the load that tractor is hauling,"
my dad says, pointing to a huge machine.
"Kind of like my brother," Justin says,
holding his nose.
Mrs. Daniels picks up Danny
and takes him off to change him.

Justin and his dad go to ride the roller coaster.

I, Amber Brown, do not like the roller coaster.

My parents and I walk toward the merry-go-round.

My parents aren't talking.

I, Amber Brown, talk a lot to make up for the quiet.

"You know, when you are my size,

you see a lot of kneecaps and rear ends."

"Amber." My mom laughs. "That's not very polite."

"But it's very true," I say.

My dad kneels down

until he's about my size and looks around.

"You're right, Amber. Sarah, take a look.

Knees and rears."

My mom looks down at both of us and joins us.

This is the best time we've all had together

since the vacation started.

They stand up and I am left alone

in a world of knees and rears.

We get to the merry-go-round.

I want us all to sit together in the sleigh.

"Let's leave that for the little kids," Mom says.

Mom and Dad get on separate animals.

I get on a lion and pretend to lie down on it.

"Look! I'm lying on a lion . . . and I'm not lying . . .

I'm telling the truth."

"And our animals are all on a line,"

Mom says, laughing.

The merry-go-round starts and I pretend
to be Amber, Queen of the Jungle.

The merry-go-round stops and we all get off.

Neither of my parents looks at the other.

Neither is saying anything.

Maybe that's better than fighting,

but it's definitely not perfect.

"We're back," Justin says, coming up

with the rest of the Daniels family.

"Hot dogs," Justin says, pointing to a booth.

We all get hot dogs.

I name mine Rover and then I can't eat it.

My dad eats Rover.

I'll never name a hot dog again.

Then Danny grabs Justin's hand and points.

"Airplane. We ride."

I want to ride with Justin,

but sometimes he has to do things with Danny.

They get into their plane first.

Then I get into the plane behind them

with a little girl who doesn't have a partner.

Justin turns and yells,

"Boys against the girls. It's a race!"

Sometimes he is very silly.

They're in front. They're going to win.

The ride starts.

The planes leave the ground.

Faster . . . faster . . . the planes tilt to the side.

Faster . . . faster . . . the planes tilt a little more.

The little girl keeps going, "Varoom . . . beep, beep."

The planes start to slow down.

As each one reaches the platform, kids get off.

Justin and Danny get off ahead of us.

I just know that he's going to say he won.

I take a close look.

Justin does not look happy, even though he "won."

In fact, he looks very unhappy.

He has throw-up all over him.

Danny has throw-up coming out of his mouth
and all over his clothes.

Mrs. Daniels takes one look at them and says,

"Let's go back to the car and get a change of clothes . . .

and no more food for either of you."

"We'll be back soon," Mr. Daniels yells

over to my parents. They wave and nod.

Mom and Dad look like they are having a big talk.

They are not smiling.

I walk over to my parents.

They don't see me.

I, Amber Brown, see and hear them.

They have angry voices.

I, Amber Brown, hate angry voices,

especially from my mom and dad.

If they are going to fight,

I am going back to the car with the Danielses.

I walk away.

They still don't see me.

I keep walking.

I see a lot of knees and rears.

I can't remember how to get to the car.

I don't see anything that I remember.

I am getting scared.

This is a very big fair.

I am getting more scared . . . and more upset.

I am very lost.

I want my mom and dad . . . and I want them now.

I start to cry.

Tears are coming down my face

and gunk is coming out of my nose.

I, Amber Brown, don't even have a tissue.

I see a family eating at a picnic table.

I go over and ask them where the cars are.

The mom asks me if I am lost.

I nod and cry more.

The dad says,

"Wait here. I'll go and get some help."

The mom takes out a tissue and wipes my eyes.

She gives me one and I wipe my nose.

The dad comes back with a policeman.
"We'll take you to the lost-and-found tent,"
the policeman says. "Don't worry.
We'll find your family."
I thank the family and wave good-bye.

The policeman takes me to a tent.

"Will the parents of Amber Brown please come
to the lost-and-found tent by the front entrance,"
a lady says over a loudspeaker.

In a few minutes, my mom and dad rush in.

They pick me up and hug me.

I'm crying. My mom is crying . . .

and I think my dad is trying not to cry.

"I was so scared," we all say at once.

Mom sniffles. "Amber, honey,

we thought you were with the Danielses.

When they came back without you,

we were so worried. We've been looking

everywhere for you."

"You were fighting," I said.

"So I went to look for them."

My mom and dad look at me

and then at each other

and then back at me.

They say how sorry they are

and hug me all over again.

The Danielses rush over.

We hug . . . except for Justin.

He just makes a face and I make a face back.

Then our families make plans to meet in an hour.

The Danielses go to the farm machines.

We go to the game booths.

I hold hands with my mom and dad

and think about being so happy

that it will spread to them.

"Look," Dad says. "Basketball.

I used to be very good at this."

We walk to the booth.

My father puts money down

and picks up a basketball.

One ball in.

Two balls in.

Three in and he wins.

I jump up and down.

For my prize I pick a big, fluffy pencil.

My dad plays again.

He wins again.

This time he picks the prize.

It's a teddy bear holding a heart.

Dad gives it to Mom.

They are smiling at each other,

and that makes me happy.

We play more games.

I, Amber Brown, throw coins and win two goldfish.

Mom, Dad and I all play the squirt game.

Some big boy wins.

A little girl cries because she loses.

I, Amber Brown, give her one of my goldfish.

I am an only child who will be happy

with an only goldfish.

The little girl is so happy.

So am I.

Today a Fair Day

turned into an almost-perfect day.

Get Ready for Second Grade, Amber Brown

The good news is that I, Amber Brown,

am going to be a second-grader.

The bad news is that Mrs. Wilson,

the second-grade teacher,

had to quit two weeks ago.

Her husband got a new job and they moved.

Anyone who was ever a second-grader

LOVED Mrs. Wilson

and said she was a great teacher.

She used to smile at me in the hall.

Now there's going to be a new teacher.

I don't know her.

She doesn't know me.

What if she doesn't like me?

I try not to think about it.

In just an hour I will find out

who the second-grade teacher is.

Right now I will get ready for school.

On my bed are all my school supplies:

new pens and pencils, a new notebook,

and my lucky pen with purple feathers.

I unzip my new teddy-bear backpack.

My aunt Pam sent it to me.

She said that it's an "Enjoy Second Grade

Present."

I named him Bear Lee.

His full name is Bear Lee Brown

because he is barely brown,

and he is barely ready for second grade.

Just like me.

I put everything in my backpack and zip it up.

"Bear Lee," I say, "you are so special.

Everyone is going to like you

except Hannah Burton.

But don't worry. She is mean to

a lot of people, especially me."

"Amber," my mom calls upstairs.

"It's time for breakfast."

I pick up Bear Lee and look in the mirror.

I'm wearing my new clothes.

On my knee is a scab.

It is almost ready to fall off.

I named it Scabulous.

Bear Lee, Scabulous, and I are ready.

Second grade, here we come!

Breakfast.

Mom and Dad have breakfast with me.

"You look beautiful," Dad says.

I smile at him.

"You look smart,"

he continues.

"You look like everybody

will want you to be their best friend."

Mom puts a bowl of cereal in front of me.

"I know that this is going to be
a great year for you," she says.

I, Amber Brown, know
that they are just saying that
because they are my mom and dad.

We finish our breakfast.

There's a knock on the door.

It's Justin, my best friend from next door.

He is wearing his new Roboman backpack.

63

My dad is driving Justin and me to school.

Justin says, "This year

I am going to tell chicken jokes."

I just look at him.

"Why did the chicken

cross the playground?" he asks.

I think about it. "To get to second grade?"

He makes a face. "No, silly.

To get to the other slide."

My father laughs and so do I.

We get out of the car and go to the playground.

That's where second-graders meet

before school starts.

Jimmy Russell and Bobby Clifford

are wrestling on the ground

in their brand-new school clothes.

Vinnie Simmons is showing everyone
the snake tattoo on his arm.
Even though he tells everyone it is real,
I can tell that it's not.

I stick my finger in my mouth to get it wet.

I ask Vinnie to let me look at the tattoo.

I touch it with my wet finger.

Some of it comes off.

I don't say anything, but I, Amber Brown,

know for sure that the tattoo is not

on Vinnie's arm forever.

Vinnie knows I know.

He sticks out his tongue at me.

Gregory Gifford and Freddie Romano
are showing each other the tricks
that they have learned over the summer.
Gregory can whistle, standing on his hands.
Freddie can recite fifteen state capitals
and do armpit music at the same time.

The girls are talking about the new teacher.

Alicia Sanchez says that her name is Ms.
Light.

"I hear that she really wants to teach
high school students," Alicia says.

"I hear that she calls second-graders
'knee biters,'" Naomi Schwartz adds.

Tiffany Schroeder holds on to
her good-luck Barbie doll.

"I'm scared," she says.

"I want Mrs. Wilson to come back."

Hannah Burton joins our group.

She looks at my backpack.

"How baby, Amber. A second-grader

shouldn't wear a baby backpack

that looks like a teddy bear."

I am not going to let Hannah

ruin second grade for me.

I ignore Hannah Burton.

Naomi and Alicia put their animal backpacks

down next to Bear Lee and look at Hannah.

She shrugs and mumbles, "Babies."

My class talks about Ms. Light

and the things that we are worried about.

I wasn't so worried until we all started talking.

What if she gives seven hours of homework?

What if she gets really upset

if we color outside the lines?

What if she doesn't give out bathroom passes?

What if she's an alien from some foreign planet?

The bell rings.

It's time to meet Ms. Light.

We all go inside to Room 2.

Ms. Light is waiting for us at the door.

She doesn't look like any teacher

I've ever seen before.

She looks like a high school kid

or a baby-sitter.

She's wearing a denim dress.

There are all sorts of patches and pins on it—

school buses, pens, pencils,

chalkboards, chalk, books, paper. . . .

And she's got on earrings

that are shaped like lightbulbs . . .

and they light up.

I get it . . . Ms. Light.

Lightbulbs.

She smiles and says
"Hello" and "Welcome"
to each of us as we go in.
She even says hello to Bear Lee.
I'm beginning to think
that Ms. Light might be okay.

The entire room is decorated.

We go to the seats

where our names are written

on cardboard cutouts of lightbulbs.

I'm sitting with Fredrich Allen.
I hope that over the summer
he stopped picking his nose.

I'm sitting with Justin Daniels.

Hooray.

I'm sitting with Hannah Burton.

Yuck.

Hannah looks at my name

on the cardboard lightbulb.

"Amber Brown. What a sap you are.

Ugh. You probably don't even know

that amber comes from tree sap that gets hard.

Sometimes there are things

like spiders and bugs in it."

I know she is right about that.

My mom gave me a book about amber

and my dad gave me an amber pendant

with a little fly in it.

Hannah makes a face at me.

That's it.

I say, "Look, Hannah BURPton. Stop it."

Fredrich Allen says,

"Hannah Burpton."

Justin starts singing,

"Unhappy Burpton to you."

Ms. Light stands at the front of the room.

"Welcome to second grade,"

she says, and smiles at us.

"This is going to be such

an exciting school year.

We are going to learn new things

about the world and ourselves."

She continues,

"As you know, my name is Ms. Light.

Do you know what the word 'light' means?"

I raise my hand quickly.

I want to be the first person

to answer a question in second grade.

Everyone else has a hand raised.

Ms. Light chooses Fredrich.

"Light is a kind of energy," he says.

Fredrich Allen is very smart.

Ms. Light beams at him.

I guess that makes it a Light beam.

She says, "Absolutely right.

Light helps us to see things.

Most of our light comes from the sun.

Some of our light comes from the moon.

We get light from electricity

when we flick a switch."

Justin pretends to put his finger

in a make-believe socket.

"ZZZZZZZZZZing."

Ms. Light nods at him.

"That can really happen. . . .

Electricity can be very powerful."

"Wow," we all say.

She grins at me. "Amber. Do you know

what your name has to do

with the word 'electricity'?"

I shake my head no.

She continues,

"The word 'electricity' comes

from the word 'electron.'

Electricity is flowing electrons.

The Greek word for 'electron' is . . ."

Everyone looks at me.

"Amber," Ms. Light says.

I light up.

I, Amber Brown, am so happy.

I guess now that I know about electricity,

I can say that I am all charged up.

Turning to Justin, I grin.

He gives me a thumbs-up. "Way to go."

I look at Hannah Burton.

I smile and cross my eyes.

Ms. Light continues,

"I want all of you to have lots of energy
to learn and to grow.
I, Ms. Light, want to help you
shine as students.

"From now on," she says,
"you are going to be the group
known as the Bright Lights."
We all grin.

Next, Ms. Light gives us all of the rules
we will follow in second grade.

We will be respectful

We will be on time

We will do our work

Then she picks up a book from her desk

and goes to her rocking chair.

She starts reading us a book.

It's a chapter book. Hooray!

By the end of the year,

I, Amber Brown, am going to be able

to read a chapter book all on my own.

And next year, when I go to third grade,

I'm going to tell the new second-graders

that they don't have to be scared.

I, Amber Brown,

am ready for second grade.

What a Trip, Amber Brown

"**I** scream. You scream. We all scream for ice cream."

Justin and I sing over and over again.

Danny just screams.

"Ice cream! Ice cream! Ice cream!"

Danny is only three. He is Justin's little brother.

"That's enough," Mom says.

We are going on vacation for two whole weeks—

I, Amber Brown, my mom,

Justin, who is my best friend, Danny,

and their mom, Mrs. Daniels.

Our dads are coming up on the weekend.

That's when their vacations start.

We're almost in the Poconos.

That's where the house is.

"Poke a nose." Justin pretends

to poke me in the nose.

"Poke a nose."

I, Amber Brown, poke back.

"Ice cream in the nose." Danny giggles behind us.

"Justin and Amber, you are going to be second-graders in a few weeks," my mom says. "I expect you to be more grown-up. You know that the Poconos is an area in Pennsylvania. Now settle down until we get there."

Justin and I make blowfish faces at each other.

Then we hear a really disgusting sound behind us.
We can't turn around. We are wearing seat belts.
We can't see anything, but we sure can smell it.

Mrs. Daniels pulls off the road.

She cleans Danny up.

Justin and I do not poke our noses,

we hold them. The van smells yucky.

We drive some more. Then Mom says,

"Turn right—we're almost there!"

We drive up to a big white house.

"We're here!" My mom sounds very happy.

Justin and I jump out and run around.

There's a tree with a swing.

Behind the fence we find a swimming pool.

This is going to be one amazing-great vacation—

as soon as we get unpacked!

I, Amber Brown,

am the fastest unpacker in the world.

In just seven and three-quarter minutes,

all of my things are put away.

Justin knocks, comes in, and looks around.

"You are so lucky not to have to share

your room with a puke-head brother."

Then he says, "Come on, slowpoke.

Let's go outside. If you don't hurry up,

I'm going to have to poke a slow in the poke-a-nose."

"Justin Daniels," I say,

"we just got here a few minutes ago."

"Well, I finished unpacking and

I have been waiting for you, Amber."

"First, I have to see your room," I say.

I want to find out how Justin has become

the fastest unpacker in the world.

I find out.

Justin Daniels is the messiest unpacker in the world.

We go downstairs and our moms give us bananas.

Justin and I pretend to be monkeys.

We scratch under our arms.

We run around.

We find a tree house . . .

we can pretend it's a monkey house.

The pool . . . we can be whales.

An animal with antlers watches us from the woods.

"Oh, dear—a deer," I say.

"Maybe it belongs to Santa and it's on vacation."

Justin starts singing,

"Rudolph the red-nose reindeer . . ."

And then he hits himself in the nose.

"That's why his nose is red . . .

because he is a poke-a-nose."

The deer leaves.

"Justin," I say, "let's have a sleep-out."

We've had sleep-overs, but NEVER a sleep-out.

He jumps up and down. "Great idea!"

Now all we have to do is convince our parents.

"It's okay if your father will sleep out with you,"
my mom says.

"Ask your dad when he calls tonight,"
Justin's mom tells him.

"Let's go swimming in the pool," Danny says.

Actually, Justin and I call it the swimming "ool"

because our moms told us

that there must not be any pee in the pool.

I hope that they keep reminding Danny.

"Splash!" Danny says, jumping into the water.

Danny has been able to swim

since he was a baby. So has Justin.

I, Amber Brown, am afraid to swim.

But I like being in the pool

as long as my feet touch the bottom and

I wear a life jacket.

Justin swims back and forth. He splashes me.

"Stop that," I say.

Justin doesn't.

He splashes me again.

Water goes up my nose.

"Submarine attack," Justin shouts.

He ducks down and comes up.

He sprays a mouthful of water at me.

"I said STOP!" I yell.

"Scaredy-cat baby." He sticks out his tongue.

"I'm not a baby."

I splash him.

He splashes back.

Now a whole gallon of water goes up my nose.

I cough. The water comes out of my nose.

Justin gets out and does a cannonball.

SPLASH!

I, Amber Brown, am totally mad.

His mom yells at him.

I, Amber Brown, am glad.

Wait until we're on dry land at our sleep-out.

When a giant grizzly bear attacks

I will save us, and Justin Daniels will have to say

that I, Amber Brown,

am the bravest person in the world.

Until then, I will not talk to him.

I, Amber Brown, am staying in my room, reading.

I am not talking to Justin.

I am not talking to my mom,

because she said that I should talk to Justin.

I look out my window and see the "ool,"

which is now probably a pool because of Danny.

I hate not talking to people.

But I've told everyone that I am mad.

There's a knock on the door.

"Who's there?" I ask.

"Boo."

It's Justin's voice.

I say nothing.

He repeats, "Boo."

"Two boos make a boo-boo,

and that's what you made . . .

a boo-boo on our friendship," I say.

"Amber. Come on," he pleads. "Boo."

"Boo who?" I finally say.

He opens the door.

"You don't have to cry. I'm sorry," he says.

Justin makes a fish face at me.

"I don't want to see anything that has to do
with water right now."

I fold my arms in front of me.

Justin gets down on his hands and knees

and makes puppy-dog sounds.

"Roll over. Play dead," I say.

He does.

Then he crawls over, licks my hand,

and lies down again.

I can't help myself.

I scratch him on his tummy like he's a dog.

It's hard to stay angry at Justin.

I, Amber Brown, am so excited.

So is Justin Daniels.

Our dads are here and as soon as it gets dark,

we are going to have a sleep-out.

Danny is not as excited as we are.

He has to stay in the house with our moms.

We told him he is having a "sleep-in,"

but he's no dope.

He knows that's just a way of saying,

"You're a baby and can't do

what the big kids are doing."

Justin and I have made a pile of things

that we really need.

Our dads are putting up the tent.

Our moms are packing the "grub."

Justin and I have already packed

some of our own grub.

It starts to get dark.

Justin's father comes back to the house.

"The tent's ready."

He has a bump on his head

from the tent falling over on him.

Justin and I jump up.

Danny yells, "I want to go."

"No," Justin and I say together.

Danny falls to the ground

and has a major temper tantrum.

We grab our things and head for the tent.

We can still hear Danny yelling.

My father is standing by the tent.

He is on his cell phone.

"Mike. Please tell the client

that I will be in touch Monday morning."

I drop some of the camping stuff on his foot.

"Oops."

My father moves his foot and keeps talking.

"Dad," I say.

"This is your vacation. It's our vacation."

He looks down at me.

I give him that look that says,

"I am your daughter . . . your only child. . . .

Please oh please . . . do this for me."

He says, "Good-bye. Talk with you on Monday.
I have some camping on my calendar right now."
On Monday, I will give him that look again.

We put everything away and then have dinner.

Justin and I make hot-dog kebabs with

onions, little tomatoes, and marshmallows.

We all sit around singing songs and TV ads.

Then the ghost stories start.

Our dads can tell some very scary stories.

I don't know about Justin's tummy . . .

but mine is beginning to hurt.

I don't know if it's the kebabs

or the scary stories.

It's getting darker.

The lightning bugs are flashing.

I wonder what animals are out at night

in the Poconos.

"Time to go to sleep," my dad says.

Just before I get into my sleeping bag,

Justin says, "We'd better check to make sure

there are no snakes in our bags."

I, Amber Brown, check very carefully.

Then I get into my sleeping bag.

Our fathers get into their bags.

They go to sleep very quickly.

They snore very loudly.

It's hard to go to sleep

with two noses snoring at once.

I keep hearing sounds outside.

I, Amber Brown, am getting very nervous.

"Amber," Justin whispers.

"Do you hear that noise?"

I listen.

At first I hear nothing

and then I hear a tiny

"*Grrrrrrrrrrrrrrrr.*"

It's a grizzly bear.

I just know it.

I remember how brave I thought I would be

if a grizzly bear attacked us.

Well, duh, I'm scared of the grizzly bear, too.

"*Grrrrrrrrrrrrrrrr.*" I hear it again.

I see Justin put his head inside his sleeping bag.

I do the same in mine.

I hear someone laughing.

It does not sound like a grizzly-bear laugh.

It sounds like a Danny Daniels giggle.

I poke my head out of the sleeping bag.

It is Danny, and he doesn't have any clothes on.

Danny's father wakes up, reaches over,

grabs his little boy, and tickles him.

Then he puts a shirt on him.

We weren't attacked by a grizzly bear . . .

we were attacked by a bare Danny.

"I snucked out," he says.

Mr. Daniels has his arms around Danny.

He looks happy to be there.

We take a vote.

Danny gets to stay with us.

My dad phones the house to let our moms know.

Our moms come out and join us.

I, Amber Brown, already know

that there is no place like home.

Now I, Amber Brown, know

that there is no place like tent.